BUT IN THE TWENTY-FIRST CENTURY, THE WORLD HAS BECOME MUCH MORE COMPLICATED.

OUR HOMES ARE GUARDED BY BURGLAR ALARMS AND CCTV.

WE BUY FOOD FROM THE SUPERMARKET INSTEAD OF CHASING IT.

WE HAVE SPECIAL HEAT-SEEKING CAMERAS TO FIND MISSING PEOPLE.

HUMAN BEINGS HAVE BECOME A LOT CLEVERER.

SO HAVE DOGS...

This city dog pound may look like an ordinary home for stray dogs, but...

...deep under the pound is something far from ordinary: the secret headquarters of the famous

HEROIC HOUNDS WHOSE PAW-POSE IN LIFE IS TO SAVE HUMANS IN DISTRESS

And the Action Station, home to their fabulous machines.

But just at the moment, everything is quiet in the Action Station – the Action Dogs are out on a mission...

1 SOMEWHERE OVER THE BAY

"Sally, stop dripping!" growled Murdoch.

The Action Dogs were in their fast patrol boat, the *Dog Paddle*, heading back to base from their latest rescue. It hadn't all gone according to plan.

"You're getting water all over the controls," complained Murdoch.

"We're all soaking," moaned Benji.

Rascal shivered. "Ice cold water made me froze – now I'm chilled from nose to toes."

"Stop being so wet," Spike said.

"It's all right for you," said Sally crossly. "You were in here, steering. You're the only one of us who didn't get dumped in the sea when that boat we were trying to rescue turned over." Everyone looked at Benji.

"Oh, no?" said Murdoch. "Who pulled the rubber bung out of the bottom of the boat?"

"The boat was half full of water," whined Benji. "I thought opening the bung would let it out."

"But it didn't, did it?" snapped Murdoch. "It let more water in."

"Never mind," said Sally soothingly. "We got the family from the boat to dry land safely, and we even managed to save the boat – once we'd put the bung back." Then she groaned. "Still, just look at my fur – yeuch! I'm sorry guys, there's nothing for it. I'm going to have to give myself a really good shake."

Sally stared at him. "What? Why?"

"We're in the *Dog Paddle*," Murdoch reminded her. "Ye're surrounded by hundreds of screens, switches and delicate electronic instruments. If ye go shaking water over all that gear, ye could cause untold damage! Ye'll just have to wait until we're back at base before ye can get dry..."

Spike leaned forward to push buttons. "At least you'll not have long to wait. We're nearly there. Yapper's sending out a smokescreen so we can get back to the Action Station without being seen."

The radio squawked in reply. *"Spike, this is Janet. Welfare Officer Brick just called. He's on his way over. Snap inspection. He wants you all in the yard for a roll call, right away."*

"You're kidding!" said Sally. "Will we have time to get dry?"

"You'll barely have time to get out of uniform," Janet told her. *"We'll use Yapper's dummy like we usually do so he can stay in the Listening Post – I'm afraid the rest of you will have to turn up as you are."*

2 A SECRET VALLEY IN TIBET

Katnip, Katmanchew's most trusted servant, bowed as he entered into the presence of his master, the most evil cat in the world.

But when he raised his eyes, even Katnip's legendary cool deserted him.

Katnip cleared his throat. "Indeed, master. Arc you – ahem – feeling quite yourself today?"

The evil crime lord chuckled. "Fear not, faithful minion. I am not, as our disgusting canine enemies would put it, losing my marbles. Nor have I gone soft. I am merely taking this opportunity to try out my new secret weapon."

Katnip looked around, puzzled. "Secret weapon, master?"

"Yes, Katnip. A weapon so diabolical that its use will put all my previous evil schemes in the shade. I refer, of course, to..."

Katnip said carefully, "That is a patio heater, master."

The feline fiend chuckled. "Not so, devoted slave. It is a *katio* heater – or to be precise, a small model of the deadly device I have created to fulfil my wicked plans."

Katnip was still puzzled. "I am afraid I do not see how..."

Katmanchew gave a ghastly grin. "Of course you do not. You lack my diabolical flair and villainous imagination."

Katnip bowed. "Just as you say, master. Oh, by the way, there is a call for you. From the unworthy creature whose freedom you recently arranged."

"Very good, Katnip. Put him on hold. I wish to finish my crossword." Katmanchew picked up his magazine. "Now, let me see. Five across. 'Do-gooding canines who will shortly be out of my fur for good...' Two words, six letters and four– Ah! I have it! Action Dogs!"

3 THE DOWNTOWN DOG SHELTER

"These dogs are wet!" Welfare Officer Brick peered at the dogs lined up for roll call. "Why are they wet?"

Officer Brick glared at Janet. "Don't be ridiculous," he snapped. "It hasn't rained here for three days. Something tells me these troublemaking mutts have been up to no good. I'm going to have to report this." He took out a sleek-looking smartphone.

Sally was shivering and looking miserable. "I want a shake," she muttered to Benji. "I'm catching my death of cold. How much longer is this going to last?"

Janet tried to think of something that would distract Officer Brick and take his mind off his suspicions. "Er – is that a new phone, sir?"

Officer Brick looked pleased. "As a matter of fact, it is."

Officer Brick would probably have gone on burbling about his phone for hours, but at that point Sally gave a blood-curdling howl. "It's no good!" she yelped. "I can't stand it any more!"

Welfare Officer Brick stared at his phone. He looked close to tears. "Look at my phone – water's got into it – it's useless!" He pointed a quivering finger at Sally. "A week's KP for that naughty dog!"

Janet was trying very hard not to laugh. "I'm sure I know someone who can fix your phone, sir. Come along, let's get you cleaned up."

As Janet led the unhappy Officer Brick away, the other dogs stared at Sally.

Rascal grinned at her. "Good ol' Sally, right on form – shook just like a thunderstorm!"

Benji looked worried. "Are you in trouble, Sally? What's KP?"

"Kennel Punishment," said Sally. "I'm supposed to stay in my kennel for a week. Fat chance. Janet won't make me do it and Brick never checks."

"Well, let's hope the soaking he got will keep Brick out of our hair for a while," said Spike. "Let's get ourselves dry and head down to the Listening Post. Maybe Yapper will have another mission for us."

4 THE ACTION STATION

Benji dried off as best he could and went to the Action Station. He found Murdoch already there, with Officer Brick's phone in bits on the table in front of him.

Grumbling, Murdoch bent over his work. Benji sat on a sofa and opened a book. It was about his favourite hero, the greatest canine explorer of all time – Spot of the Antarctic.

Sally came in, brushing her coat. "Has anyone seen Spike?" she asked.

Benji didn't look up from his book. "Janet asked him to go out and get a paper..."

At that moment, Spike came in.

TAKE A LOOK AT THIS!

THE INDEPENDOG
CAPTAIN CLAW ESCAPES!
CRAFTY CAT BREAKS OUT OF ALKATRAD

Benji whistled. "So Captain Claw is on the loose again."

"Aye, the old sinner," growled Murdoch. "Remember the trouble he caused us last time we met? We put him behind bars – and now our old enemy Katmanchew has got him out again, you mark my words."

Sally nodded. "I dare say you're right – but why would Katmanchew want Captain Claw?"

"Katmanchew hates water," Spike told her, "so if he's planning any skulduggery on the high seas, he'll want his old hench-cat Captain Claw to do the dirty work for him..."

He broke off as Yapper burst into the room, waving a piece of paper over his head.

5 THE BRIEFING ROOM, MOMENTS LATER
THIS IS A MAP OF THE ANTARCTIC.

Yapper continued, "This area is called the Weddell Sea. Normally, at this time of the year it's frozen over. But right now something very strange is happening."

Benji thought hard. "I suppose that means the ice in that part of the sea will melt – doesn't it?"

Murdoch rolled his eyes. "The laddie's a regular Einstein."

Yapper ignored Murdoch. "That's exactly what it means. And that's the problem. There's a survey team out on the ice..."

Sally gasped. "That sounds serious."

"It is serious," Yapper told her. "If we don't get to them fast, they'll be trying to walk on ice cubes."

"There's something funny going on here," said Murdoch darkly. "For the temperature to rise as fast as this is not natural. And if it isn't natural, something – or somebody – must be causing it."

Rascal looked blank. "Give us all some good advice – who done caused the melting ice?"

"I could make a guess," growled Spike. "There's only one *somebody* I can think of who has the technology to cause this kind of problem *and* is crazy enough to do it – Katmanchew!"

"...but before I do," mewled the villainous old sea cat, "may I say how grateful I am to you for getting me out of jail..."

"Spare me your pathetic grovelling!" Katmanchew pointed an accusing paw at the trembling pirate. "The last time I employed you, you bungled my carefully planned operation and allowed the Action Dogs to escape. The only reason I set you free from prison was to perform a task for me. Have you done so?"

"Absolutely, m-m-master," stammered Captain Claw.

"AND ALL HAVE REACHED THEIR TARGETS."
"ALL THE KATIO HEATERS HAVE DEPLOYED SUCCESFULLY..."

"...AND THE TEMPERATURE IN THE REGION IS ALREADY RISING."
"WE HAVE NOW SUBMERGED WHILE WE PREPARE THE NEXT WAVE OF MISSILES FOR LAUNCHING."

Katmanchew nodded. "Excellent, Captain. It seems that this time your efforts have not been completely useless."

Captain Claw bowed low. "I live to please you, master."

"Worthless wretch – you live only for *as long as* you please me, and don't you forget it." Katmanchew ended the call. "Katnip?"

Katnip stepped forward. "What is your evil will?"

"Prepare for my TV broadcast to all nations. Now that we have broken the ice, it's time we turned the heat up on world leaders – and on the Action Dogs!"

7 THE ACTION STATION

"I don't get it," said Benji. "If Katmanchew is behind this, why would he want to melt the ice in the Antarctic?"

"What I don't get," growled Spike, "is *how* he can be doing it!"

"I think I can help ye there." Murdoch dimmed the lights and clicked buttons on a remote control. A projector whirred and a picture appeared on the screen.

"What on earth would Katmanchew want with a submarine?" demanded Sally. "Cats hate water."

"Like Spike said, Captain Claw doesn't," Benji pointed out, "and he's just escaped from jail – probably with help from Katmanchew."

"You're right," said Sally. "There could be a connection..."

"Hey, guys..." Yapper looked up from a computer at which he had been busily punching keys.

"I just hacked into the Earthview 'eyes in the sky' system. It has satellites covering every continent on earth, 24/7. I had a look at the part of Antarctica where the temperature is rising, and look what I found."

The Chihuahua continued, "I only ask because I've never seen anything like it before, and there seem to be eight of them in the area where the ice is melting."

Murdoch snarled, "Some devilish machine of Katmanchew's, no doubt."

Spike nodded grimly. "Like I said – I'll bet a box of doggy treats to a rubber bone, that foxy fleabag is behind this."

"All right," said Sally, "I'll buy that – but we still don't know why–"

"Hold everything!" Yapper cupped a paw around the earphone of his headset. "There's a message coming through – I'm sending it to the main screen..."

Katmanchew glowered from the screen. His amplified voice echoed round the Action Station. "No doubt you have been wondering why the ice at the South Pole has begun to melt. It is all my doing. I have already deployed a number of wickedly warm katio heaters and am preparing to launch more..."

"Told you," said Spike grimly.

Sally glared at him. "Hussshhh."

Rascal shook his head. "So that's his plan, the dirty rat! That is one power-mad pussycat."

"Sea levels all over the world will rise," raved the furry master criminal. "London, New York and Venice will be drowned. Low-lying countries such as Holland, Bangladesh and Cambodia will disappear beneath the waves. To the leaders of the world, I say pay up within twenty-four hours, or face global katastrophe! Choose quickly! The heat is on! The ice has already started to melt..."

As Katmanchew's leering face faded from the screen, Spike was already rapping out orders. "We'll see about that! Murdoch, load the *Sea Dog* into the Bonecopter. Better take the Dogsled too."

Benji bounced up and down with excitement. "We're going to the Antarctic, then? Boy oh boy..."

Startled, the Action Dogs turned to see Master Yi standing in the doorway of the Action Station. The wise old Taekwondog master gazed calmly at their worried faces. "Missing something, am I?"

Sally bowed. "Master Yi, we are going to the Antarctic, land of eternal cold, where the mind becomes confused and the helpless traveller may be lost for ever in the bewildering mists, gleaming snowfields and perilous ice floes of the white, featureless landscape. Do you have any wise advice that will keep us safe on our quest?"

The Pekingese closed his eyes in meditation. For several moments, he remained deep in thought. Then, at length, he opened his eyes and spoke...

8 ON BOARD THE SUBMARINE *KATFISH*, SOMEWHERE BENEATH THE WEDDELL SEA

One of the radar operators looked up from his screen. "Sir! I'm picking something up – it seems to be a large aircraft, heading this way..."

"What?" Captain Claw rounded on the unfortunate crewman. "Impossible!"

The radar operator gulped, but held his ground. "It's there all right, sir. Bearing two-seven-zero."

Claw spun the periscope. A moment later, the hardened villain gave a wail of despair. "It's them!

That's the Bonecopter. The Action Dogs are here! What'll we do?" The terrible pirate chieftain bit his claws in panic. "Get me Katmanchew!" he howled.

Moments later, the face of the evil crime lord was gazing down at his quaking minion.

Katmanchew exploded with rage. "Of course they are, dolt! Did you think our enemies would be sitting on their paws?"

Captain Claw bit through the rim of his cap in his terror. "But what am I to do?"

"Blockhead! This is part of my plan! I knew the Action Dogs would turn up."

Captain Claw brightened. "Indeed, master?"

"Of course, fool! The Action Dogs' first duty is to help humans in distress. They will try to save the survey party stranded on the ice before they come after you."

"The fact that they will come after me is what I am worried about, master."

Katmanchew's eyes narrowed. "Do you think I would have given you a substandard submarine? The *Katfish* is virtually undetectable underwater. All you have to do is submerge, and remain hidden until they are busy with their idiotic rescue. Then you can launch the missiles with the rest of the Katio heaters, and my evil plan will be complete! One hundred billion dollars in the kitty and the Action Dogs left skating on very thin ice. When the ice breaks they will be out of Action – purrmanently."

"I hear and obey, great master!"

The cold-hearted Katmanchew ended the call.

Captain Claw turned to his crew. "Well? Didn't you hear? Dive, dive, dive! Take us down to three hundred metres!"

9 ON BOARD THE BONECOPTER, SOMEWHERE ABOVE THE WEDDELL SEA

"Look out for open water," ordered Spike.

Sally pointed. "There's a patch down there. I'm sure I saw something floating in it a minute ago, but it's gone now."

"A whale, maybe." Spike looked around the control room. "Okay, let's run over the plan one more time. Murdoch, you and I will take the *Sea Dog*, look for the *Katfish* and stop it launching any more heaters."

Murdoch nodded. "F.I.D.O."

"Then the rest of you take the Bonecopter to save the survey team. Once we've done all that we can deal with the heaters that are already out on the ice. Any questions?"

"We'll need to pick the *Sea Dog* up with the Bonecopter after the mission," said Sally. "How will we find you?"

"No problem," said Spike. "Murdoch has built

in an ultrasound transmitter. The signal will travel a long way underwater. We'll switch it on as soon as we're submerged."

"Won't the *Katfish* be able to track the transmitter, too?" asked Sally.

Murdoch shook his head. "The transmissions will sound like whale song. The receiver on the Bonecopter will be able to tell the difference, but the crew of the *Katfish* won't."

"Anything else?" demanded Spike. All the Action Dogs shook their heads. Spike nodded grimly. "Then let's do it! Sally, take us down over the hole in the ice."

SALLY TO SPIKE. READY TO DROP?
F.I.D.O.
SEA DOG AWAY!

Spike started the motors and the *Sea Dog* surged forward. "All we have to do now is to find the *Katfish* and Captain Claw."

"Aye," growled Murdoch, "but that's easier said than done. The *Katfish* will have all the latest anti-detection gear, and it's a big ocean. It'll be like looking for a needle in a haystack."

"We'd better get on with it then," said Spike.

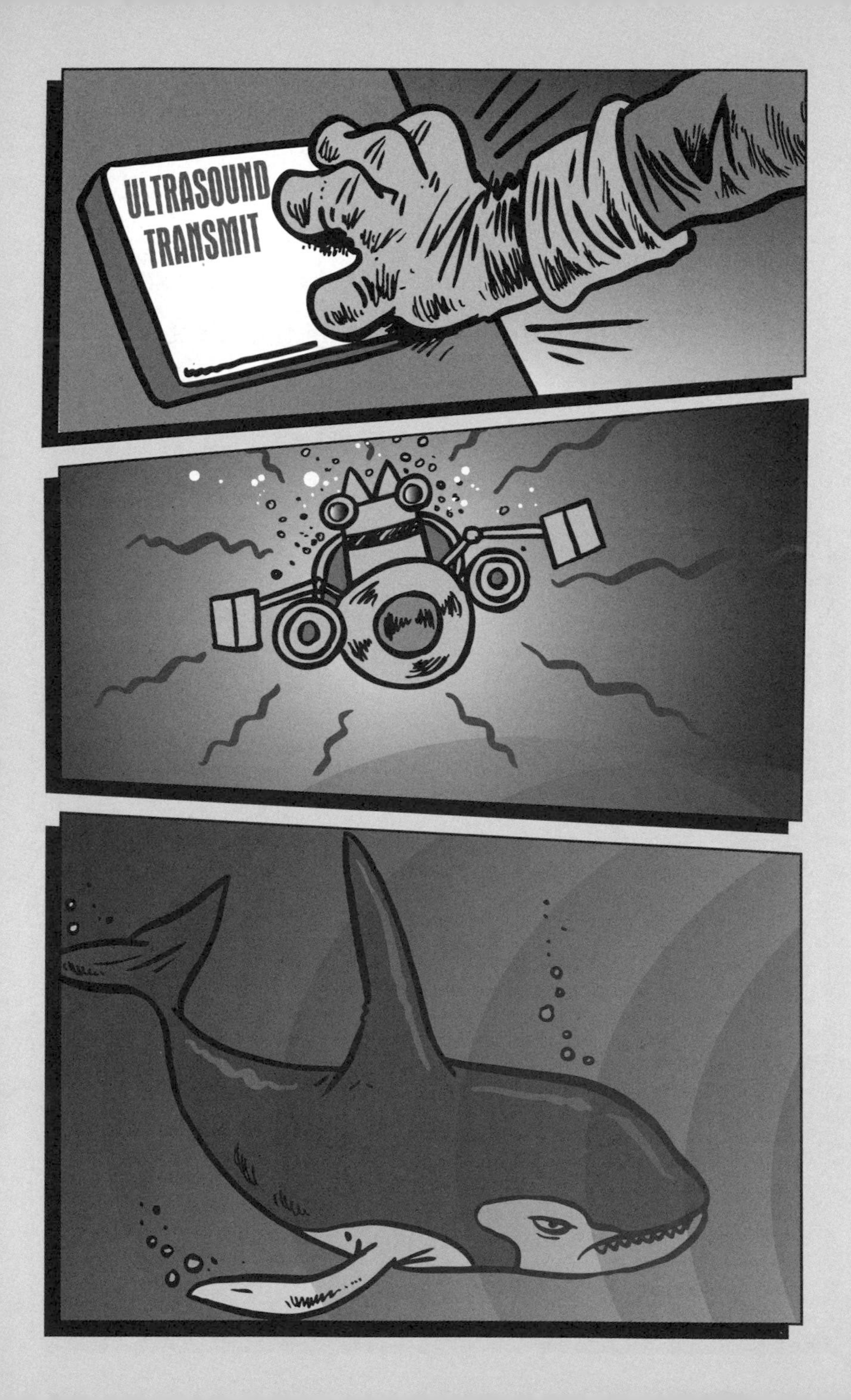
ULTRASOUND
TRANSMIT

Spike peered into the dark water. "Let's get on with the search. Start a sonar sweep. Is there anything out there?"

Murdoch stared at his screens in horror. "Aye, you could say that. Don't look now..."

10 ON BOARD THE BONECOPTER, A FEW MINUTES LATER

Sally looked worried. "I can't land on the ice floe," she said, "it's much too small. Even if I go near it, the downdraught from the rotors might turn it over or blow everyone into the sea. What's more, all the ice near here is too thin to take the Bonecopter's weight – and it's still melting. We'll have to land somewhere the ice is thicker."

Rascal groaned. "Far away will cause delay – we won't save those folks, no way."

"It's not as bad as all that," Sally told him. "We'll have to use the Dogsled."

"What?" Benji stared at Sally. "You mean, we have to pull a sled over the ice? Like huskies?"

Sally grinned. "Wait and see..."

MY MUM SAYS I'M EXCUSED FROM PULLING DOGSLEDS ON ACCOUNT OF I'M NOT STRONG ENOUGH AND I'VE GOT A VERRUCA.
PIPE DOWN, BENJI.

Sally led the way into the rear equipment bay of the Bonecopter and flicked a switch. The big doors at the back of the Bonecopter opened, and light flooded in. There was something long and thin sitting in the middle of the floor.

Sally flicked another switch. There was a rumble, and a ramp shot through the door, tilting down. At the same moment, the Dogsled slid out from under its covering, raced down the ramp, and came to rest, gleaming, on the snow.

11 OUT ON THE ICE...

A thought struck Benji. He had to shout to make himself heard over the noise of the engine and the rushing wind. "What happens when we get to the sea? The survey party are stranded on an ice floe – we'll have to cross the water to get to them."

Sally laughed. "Don't worry, this is a clever machine. It's all taken care of." She peered ahead, and her brow furrowed. She released the throttle, and the Dogsled slowed down. "Uh-oh."

"What's up?" asked Benji.

"We're coming to the edge of the snowfield. The ice is more broken here – we'll have to go carefully."

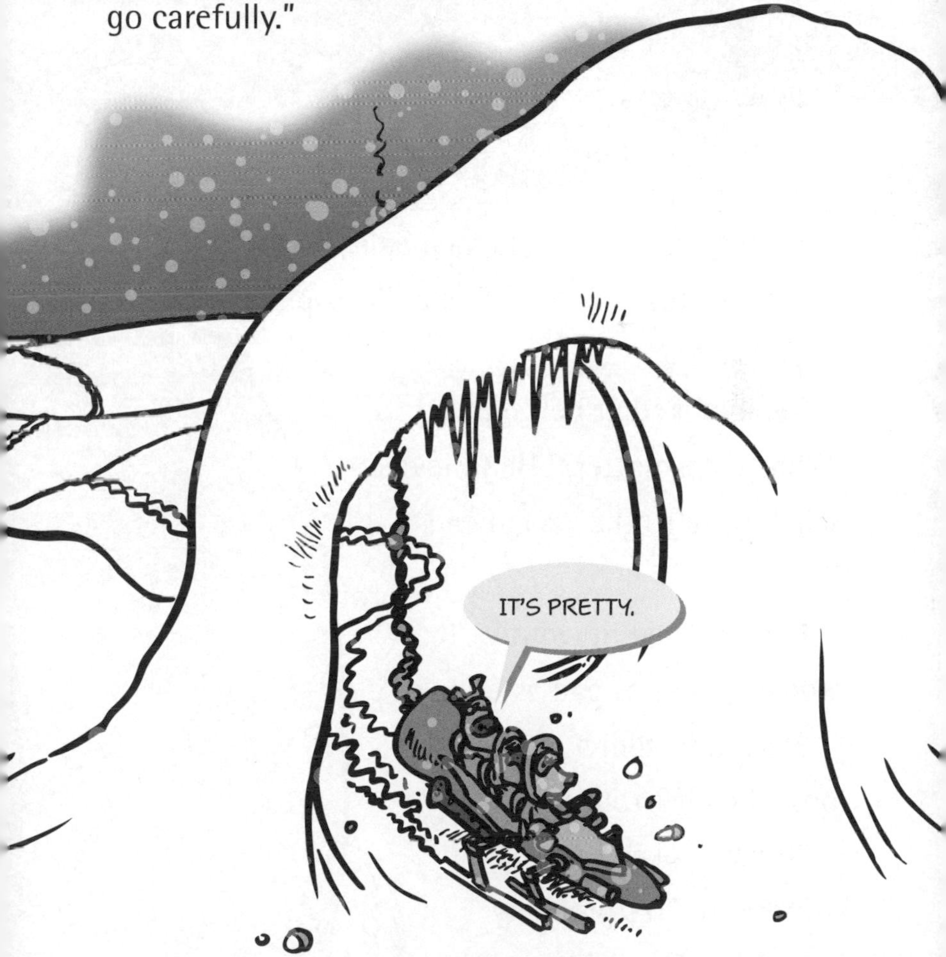

"It may be pretty," snapped Sally, "but it's slowing us up – oh, no!" She pulled up and killed the engine.

Benji looked at her, startled. "What's the matter?" He followed Sally's gaze to the way ahead. "Oh, dear."

Benji gulped nervously. "It probably isn't as bad as it looks."

Sally gave him a disbelieving look. "Really? You think?"

"It looks okay," said Benji stubbornly. "It's probably been there for years."

"Yes, but the ice around here is melting! It doesn't look to me as if it would take the weight of the Dogsled, and I'm not going to try it." Sally turned to Rascal. "Get the map out. Maybe there's a way around that won't lose us too much time."

As Sally and Rascal pawed over the map, Benji wandered off.

"Yes, look." Sally pointed. "The chasm ends just up here. It'll take a bit longer, but we can still do it. Let's go. Benji, mount up." When there was no reply, Sally raised her head. "Now where's he got to? Benji!" she called. "Where are you?"

Benji scowled. Sally was always ordering him about. "I told you," he called, "it's safe." He began to jump up and down. "See?..."

12 MEANWHILE, UNDERWATER

Spike wrestled with the controls. "They're faster than we are – we can't outrun them!"

"Why are the stupid things attacking us?" demanded Murdoch. "It's not as if we're threatening them."

"Well, they're threatening us!" Spike sent the *Sea Dog* into a dive to avoid the charge of an angry orca. "Can't you make this thing go any faster?"

"I cannae do it," moaned Murdoch, "I hav'nae got the power!"

The submersible shook as another orca swiped it with its powerful tail. "They'll sink us in a minute!" snarled Spike.

"Aye. I doubt she'll stand much more." The Scottish terrier shook his head. "We cannae take another attack!"

Murdoch stared at him. "What are ye going to do? We cannae fight them – this is an unarmed vessel."

"Wrong!" said Spike. "We don't have torpedoes and suchlike – but we do have arms! Take over the steering..."

Spike grinned. "Let's see how they like a taste of their own medicine..."

Muroch gave a yap of excitement. "Aye, that's the stuff to give 'em! Pinch their tails! Tickle 'em! That's for ye, ye cowardy custards!"

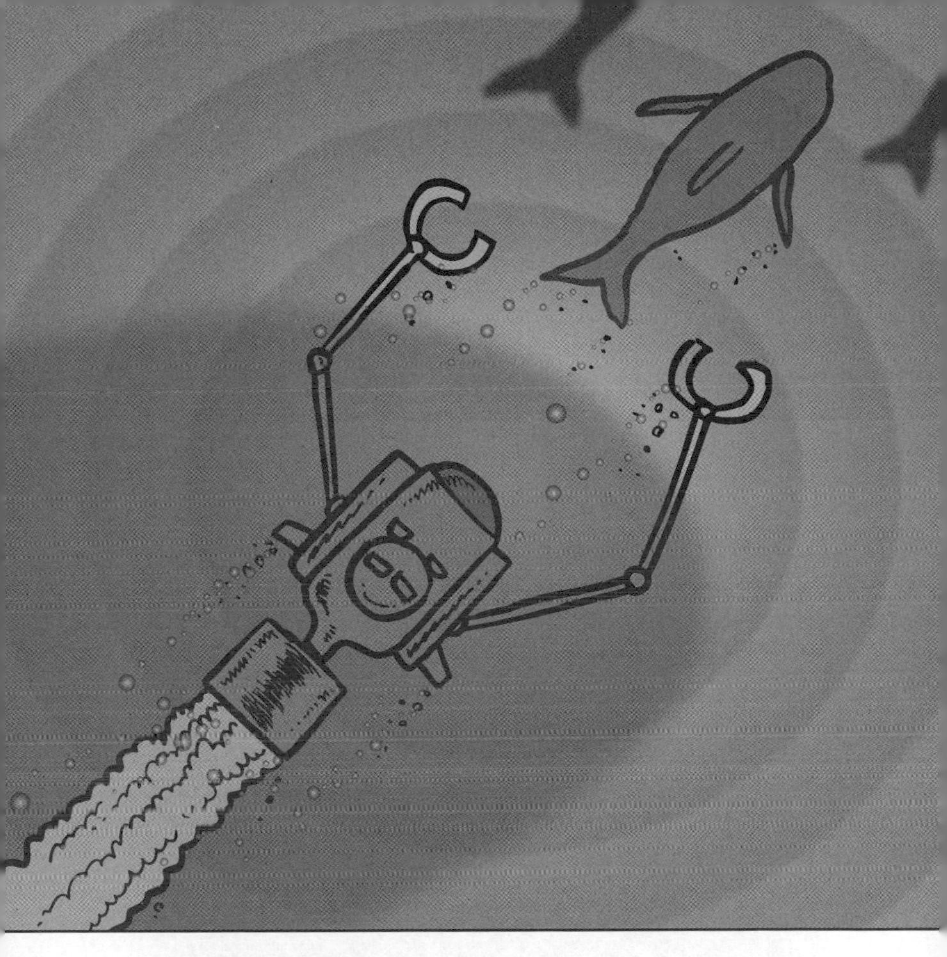

Then Murdoch looked up. "Oo-er." He tapped Spike on the shoulder. "I dinnae like to spoil your fun, but have you seen the beastie that's just come up on our tail?"

"No," said Spike, concentrating on his attempts to nip at the retreating orcas. "What is it?"

"A sperm whale!" howled Murdoch.

Spike gave him a worried look. "That's not good, is it?"

"No! Did you never hear tell of Moby Dick? A sperm whale is six times the size of an orca, and it likes nothing more that biting ships in half with its terrible, masterful jaws!"

13 BACK ON THE ICE

Benji felt as if every bone in his body was broken, but he managed to struggle to his feet, so they probably weren't. He looked round. He had clearly fallen a long way. Smooth, glistening walls of ice rose up to either side of him: they didn't look as if he'd be able to climb them. He was well and truly stuck.

But just then, he heard a voice...

Benji cupped his paws around his muzzle and yelled back, "Sally? Is that you?"

Sally's voice echoed back down to him. "Oh, thank goodness! We thought you'd fallen right through the ice!"

"I haven't, and I'm not hurt – but I can't get out!" Benji shivered. "Listen, it's my own fault I'm down here – leave me, go and rescue the survey team..."

"No!" called Sally. "We're not leaving without you. This crevasse could close – and if we went away, we might never find this place again. Hang on – we're going to get you out!"

Benji waited. For a while, nothing happened. Then...

Benji put the coat on. "Now what?"

Sally's faint call came back. "Now – stand by!"

Benji went up through the crevasse as though he was in an express elevator, until...

WELL, DON'T HANG AROUND! WE'VE GOT WORK TO DO!

But a few hundred metres away...

THE ACTION DOGS HAVE ALLOWED THEMSELVES TO BE DISTRACTED, JUST AS OUR MASTER KATMANCHEW SAID THEY WOULD.

HEAD FOR OPEN WATER. PREPARE TO SURFACE! THEN WE WILL FIRE THE MISSILES AND FINISH OFF THE ACTION DOGS.

As the gigantic whale's jaws began to close, Spike left the *Sea Dog*'s mechanical arms and made a grab for the steering controls. "Emergency power! Hold on to your breakfast!"

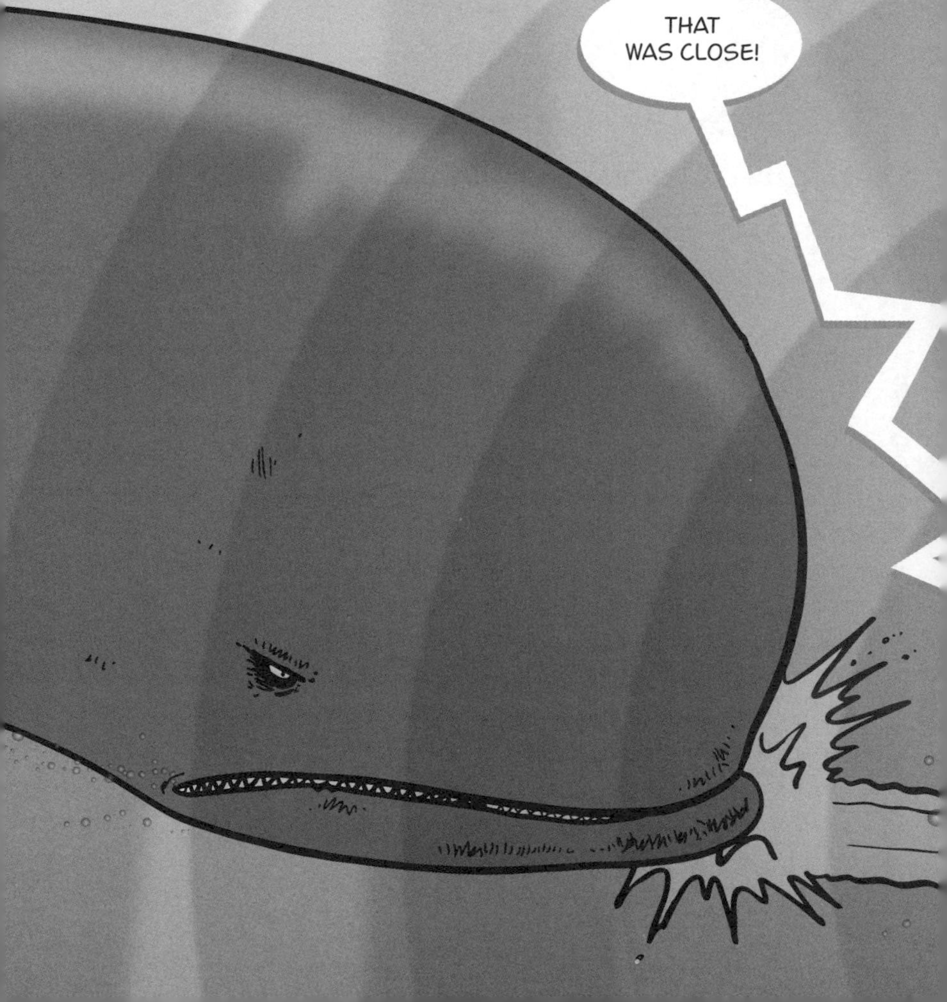

Murdoch gulped. "I thought we were goners that time!"

Spike was zig-zagging to try and stay out of the whale's reach. "I heard that whales can't swallow anything bigger than a grapefruit!"

"That's blue whales! A sperm whale will munch us up like a pair of doggy chews." Murdoch bashed himself on the forehead with a clenched paw. "I wish I knew why the whales are attacking us. I cannae think of anything that might cause such aggressive behaviour..." He opened his eyes wide, "...unless..."

"Unless what?" Spike jinked the *Sea Dog* to avoid another attack by the furious sperm whale. "Spit it out!"

"Unless – the ultrasound transmitter! I rigged it to send out a signal that sounds like whale song – that must be what's making them mad!"

SWITCH IT OFF, THEN!
AYE, AYE!

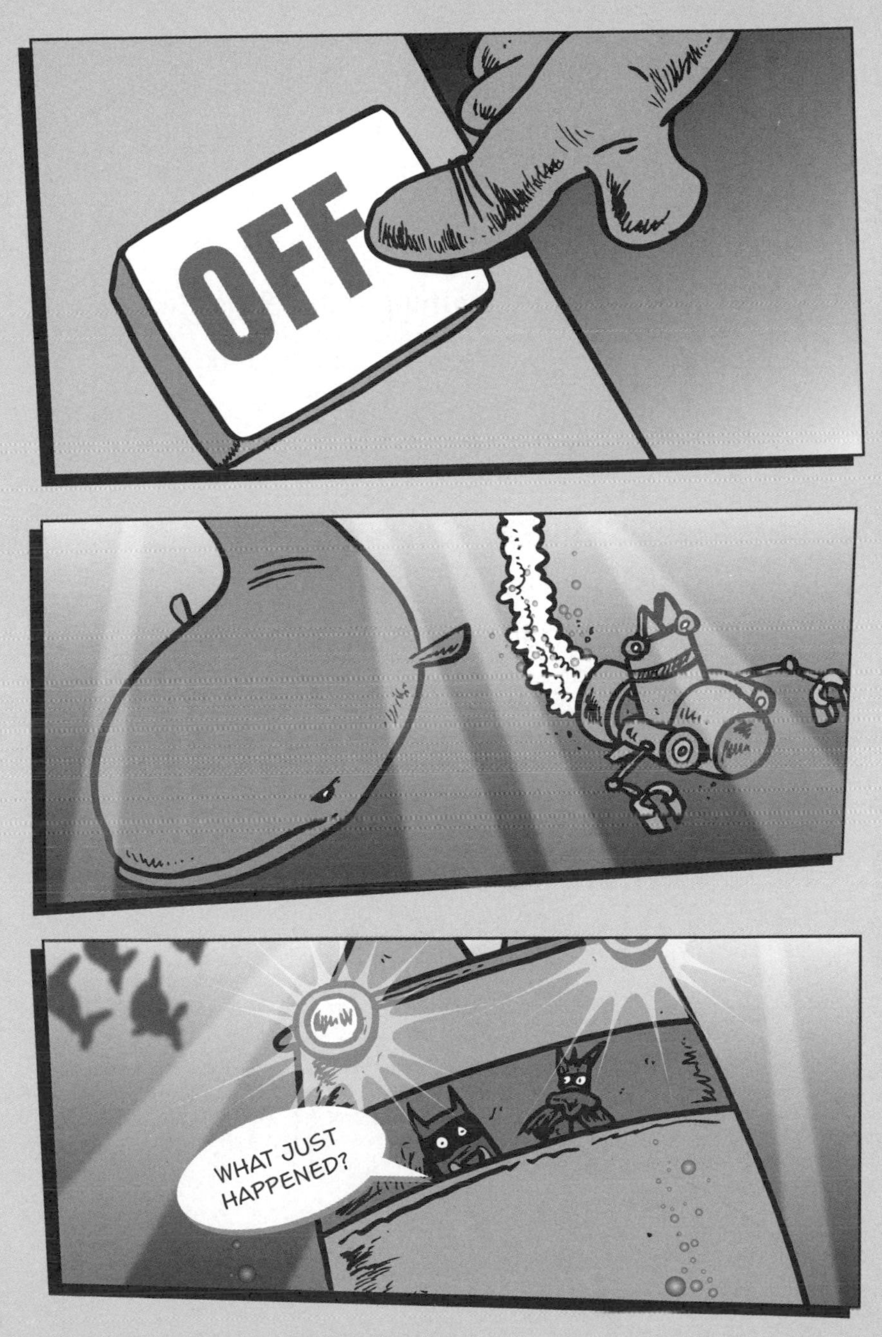
OFF
WHAT JUST HAPPENED?

Murdoch took a deep breath. "Well, ye know whales talk to each other with their songs? I tried to get our transmitter to send out a signal disguised as a whale song, but I must have accidentally hit on something that sounds like a rude message to whales – something like, 'Your mother is a walrus' or 'Come and have a go if you think you're hard enough'!"

"No wonder they were mad at us!" Spike peered into the dark water. "Anyway, if you're right, we should be safe as long as we don't use the transmitter again. All we have to do now is find the *Katfish*..."

I THINK WE JUST HAVE!

"And she's blowing her tanks," said Murdoch. "It looks like she's about to surface. If we want to stop her firin' more heaters, we hav'nae much time!"

15 UP ON THE ICE AGAIN

Sally's expression was grim as the Dogsled hurtled over the ice and snow. "I hope we're in time," she muttered.

"Me too." Benji was feeling guilty. His fall had held them up, and the detour round the crevasse had cost more time. "I hope the survey team is still alive," he muttered, nervously.

With a roar, the Dogsled shot over the top of a hill, and at last Benji could see the gap in the ice, not too far away. Sally stopped the Dogsled and reached for a pair of binoculars.

Sally put the binoculars away and gunned the engine. The Dogsled shot forward again.

As they approached the hole in the ice, Benji felt panic rising within him. He tapped Sally on the shoulder. "Er...when I asked you how we were going to get across the water to rescue the survey team, you said it was all taken care of. You never actually said how we were going to do it."

Sally gave him a fierce grin. "We're going to do it like this..."

SELECTING
HOVER MODE
COOL!

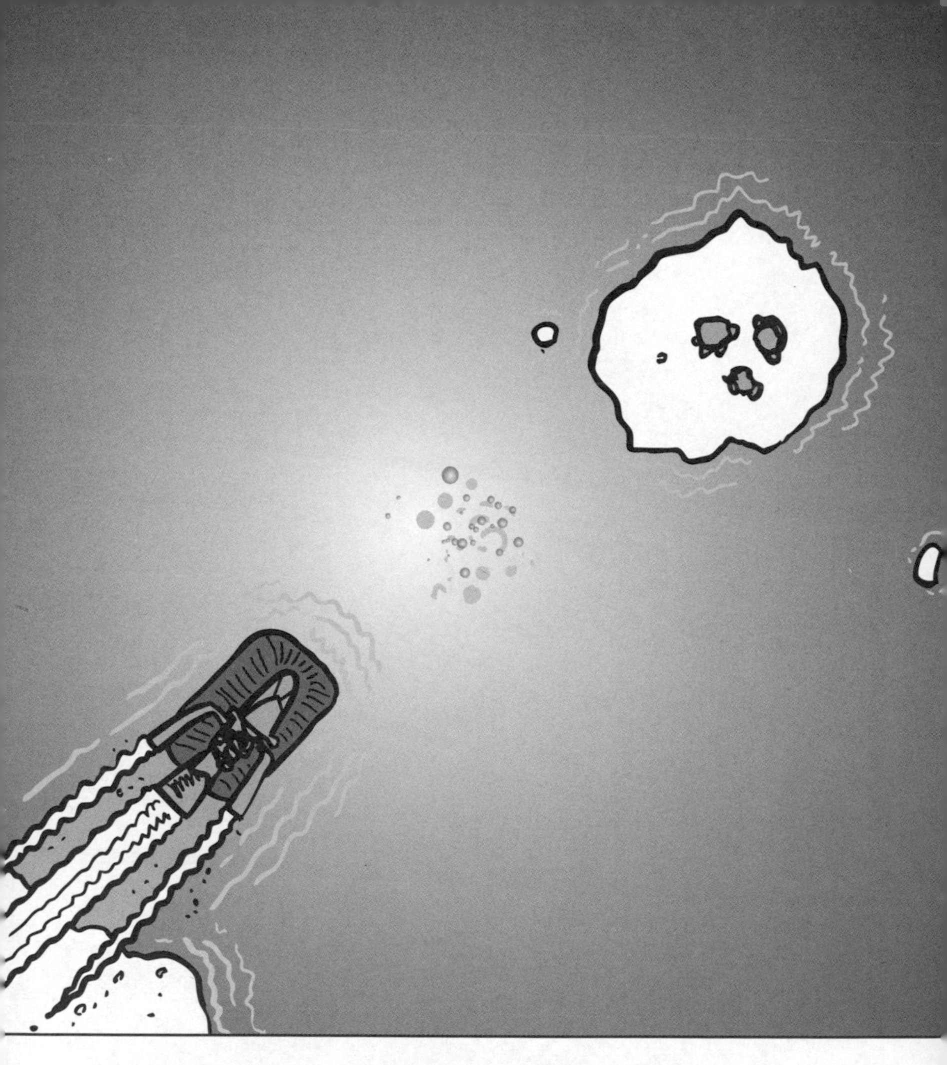

Sally leaned over the handlebars in her excitement. "We're going to make it!"

But just then...

"What's that?" Benji pointed. "Dead ahead? It looks like bubbles. It looks like..."

YIKES!
OH, NO!
DOGGONE!

AHOY THERE, ME HEARTIES! WELCOME ABOARD THE GOOD SHIP KATFISH – YOU ARE MY PRISONERS.

16 A FEW METRES AWAY

Murdoch gave a low growl. "Aye – safe in the hands of that villain! But who's to say when he'll decide to feed them to the fishes?"

Spike ground his teeth in frustration. "And in the meantime, if the *Katfish* has surfaced, that must mean they're getting ready to fire more missiles. If they succeed, they'll melt all the ice in the Antarctic!"

Murdoch slammed his paw down on the arm of his chair. "We've got to stop them!"

"Yes, but how?" snapped Spike. "Look at the size of that thing! And we have no guns, no torpedoes..."

"Aye, we need help right enough..." Murdoch broke off. "Help! That's it – we need help..."

17 ON BOARD THE SUBMARINE *KATFISH*

Captain Claw pushed his scarred face close to his captives. "Katmanchew will be pleased with me," he hissed. "Last time we met, you spoiled his plan and made me look foolish. But now... now the boot is truly on the other paw." He turned away, to stand before a communications screen on which the face of Katmanchew had appeared.

"Are the remaining missiles ready?" demanded the crime lord.

Captain Claw bowed again. "Yes, indeed, your wickedness."

"Good. Fire them, and return to base."

"Of course, deplorable one!" Captain Claw looked up, greatly daring. "And the survey team? Should I capture them, too?"

"What for, imbecile? You have no time to spare for looking after prisoners."

Captain Claw, hardened villain though he was, looked uncomfortable – but he only said, "And what of the Action Dogs, lord?"

Katmanchew smiled. "What indeed? Meddlesome mutts, it appears you have thwarted my plans for the last time."

"Don't be too sure of that, fur-face," Benji said angrily.

Katmanchew gave an evil chuckle. "Oh, but I am sure. What am I to do with you? Hmmmmm. I could throw you off my submarine, but then you could swim to safety."

Rascal gave him a defiant glare. "Swimming is, I must confess, what spaniels like me do the bes'."

"Exactly so." Katmanchew gave a tigerish grin. "But I think even you would have a problem swimming through solid ice."

Captain Claw's fur stood on end. "Surely, master, you cannot mean..."

"Oh, I certainly can mean." Katmanchew leaned forward. "Once the remaining missiles are airborne, submerge and go under the ice. Then, our guests may leave – through the airlock!"

18 ONE HORRIFIED REACTION LATER

Captain Claw stood staring at the communications screen even after his evil master's picture had disappeared.

Sally glared at him. "So this is how you treat your prisoners, you monster."

Captain Claw gave her a guilty look. "Orders is orders."

"You know perfectly well that if you put us out of the airlock while we're under the ice, we'll drown."

Captain Claw glared at Sally. "Shut up when you speak to me!" He stomped off, shouting orders.

OPEN MISSILE BAY DOORS!
SPLICE THE MAINBRACE!
PREPARE TO FIRE!
WELL, IF WE'RE ALL GOING TO THE DOGS, I MAY AS WELL TRY AND GET COMFORTABLE FIRST.

Glaring at Captain Claw, Sally stopped shaking. But Benji had an idea. He remembered some of the things he'd seen and heard over the last few hours...

"Sally," whispered Benji out of the corner of his mouth, "Rascal – both of you listen. I've got an idea. When I give the word, I want you to shake for all you're worth."

Sally stared at him. "What good will that do? Apart from getting us dry..."

"Just trust me." Benji held his breath. The cats were busy, getting ready for the missile launch...

...TWO...ONE...
FI—!
NOW! SHAKE!

19 OUTSIDE THE *KATFISH*, A FEW METRES AWAY...

MURDOCH, I HOPE YOU KNOW WHAT YOU'RE DOING.

DINNAE BOTHER ME NOW, SPIKE.

It was a long swim from the *Sea Dog* to the *Katfish*, but eventually Murdoch reached the submarine. He reached into the bag at his belt and pulled out a metal object, which he pressed against the hull.

"Uh-oh," muttered Murdoch. "I hope nobody heard that." He rested his helmet against the submarine's hull to listen for sounds of disturbance inside.

His eyes widened. "Spike!" he yelled into his suit radio. "Spike! There's a regular hullabaloo going on inside this submarine!"

Spike's voice sounded in his earphones. *"Have you attached the whatchamacallit you've been working on?"*

"Yes!"

"Then get back here, fast!"

"F.I.D.O." Murdoch pushed away from the hull and started on the long swim back.

20 MEANWHILE, INSIDE THE *KATFISH*

Captain Claw turned to an officer. "Fire those missiles!"

"I can't, sir!" wailed the officer. "All this water has crashed the computer. It's stopped the launch and shut everything down. Now it just keeps asking me for my user ID and pussword!"

Captain Claw turned on his prisoners. "Interfering fleabags! This is all your doing!" With a snarl, he drew a wicked-looking sword and charged towards Benji.

Benji gulped. He knew he'd only have one chance to get this right. As Captain Claw raised the sword, he took a step back and held out his tied paws...

Before Captain Claw could bring his sword up for another blow...

"Great, Benji," cried Sally. "Your Taekwondog is really coming on. I'd applaud, but *my paws are still tied together*!"

"Oh – sorry." Hurriedly, Benji untied Sally and Rascal.

Rascal rubbed his wrists. "Dawg, your moves are really *bad*, but pussycats are looking mad."

THWOCK!

21 A FEW MOMENTS LATER
SO MUCH FOR CAPTAIN CLAW. I WONDER HOW SPIKE AND MURDOCH ARE DOING?

Sally hauled an unconscious cat away from the submarine's radio station. "Sally calling *Sea Dog*, Sally calling *Sea Dog*. Come in, Spike. Over."

The reply came through straight away. "Sea Dog *calling Sally. What's happening? Over!*"

Sally pressed the transmit button again. "Spike, we've taken over the control room, stopped the launch and wrecked the guidance computer so Captain Claw won't be able to fire the rest of his missiles – but there are a lot more cats in this crew and sooner or later they're going to figure out there's something wrong up here, over."

"Spike calling Sally – get out of there, double-quick! Murdoch's arranged a little surprise for our friends, and you don't want to be on that sub when it happens!"

"F.I.D.O." Sally grinned at Benji and Rascal. "Okay, guys you heard that. We're busting out of here..."

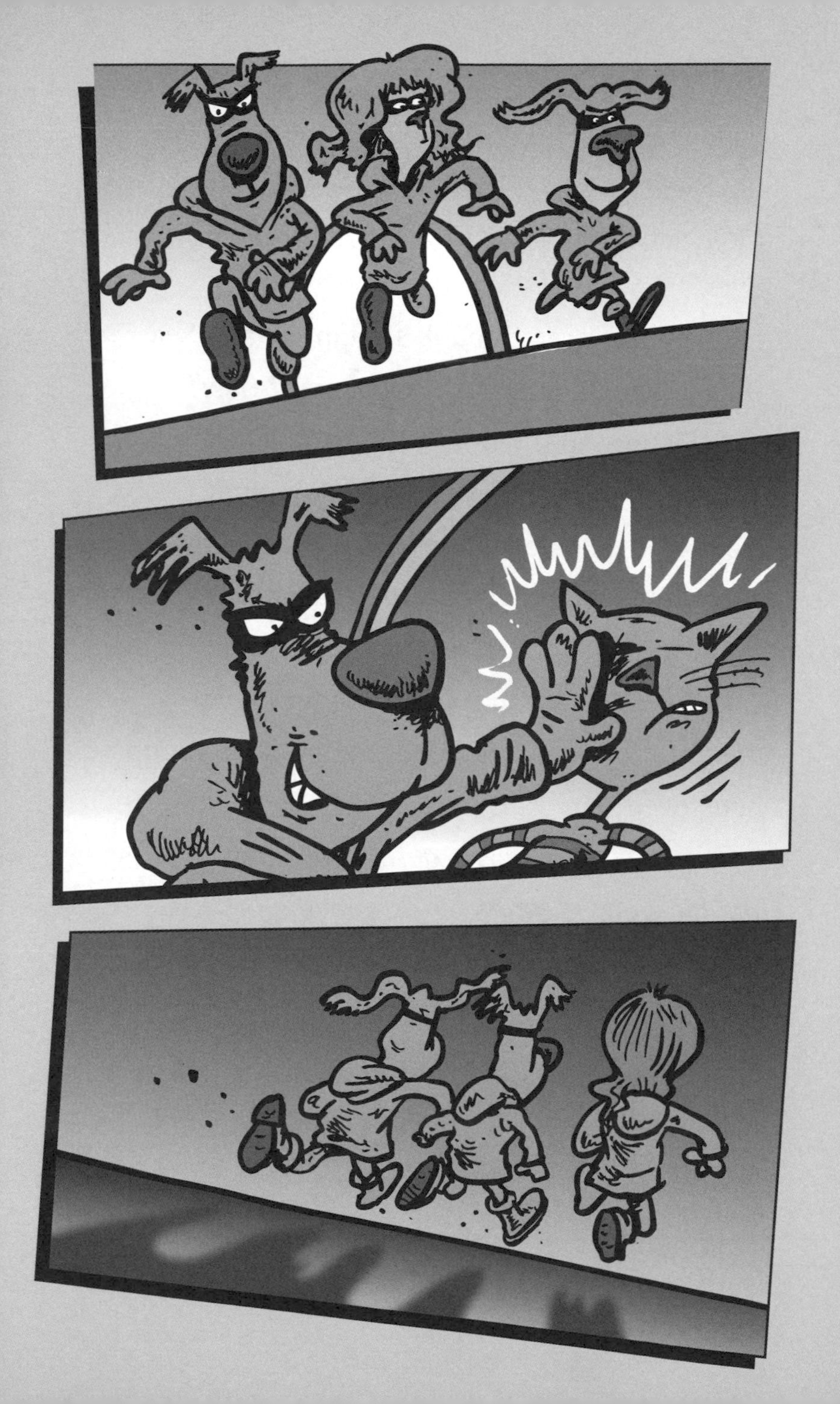

Sally was already untying the dinghy. "Let's get moving."

Rascal and Benji tumbled into the dinghy and started paddling for all they were worth...

JUST WAIT, ACTION DOGS!
I'LL POP YOUR LITTLE BOAT,
AND YOU CAN GO PLAY WITH
THE FISHES...

Inside the *Sea Dog*, Spike and Murdoch watched in horror as Captain Claw prepared to fire.

"Quick, laddie!" howled Murdoch. "Press the remote control button for the ultrasound transmitter!"

Spike stared at him. "The what?"

"The thing I stuck to the hull of the submarine – you know..."

ULTRASOUND TRANSMIT
WHAT THE…?
NO – NO! AAAAARRRGGGHHH!

Sally gaped as the orca splashed back into the sea and Captain Claw scuttled for shelter. "Is that the surprise Murdoch arranged? I've got to say – it's a doozie!"

Benji started paddling again. "Come on – let's get to the *Sea Dog*. We've saved the world, but we still have to rescue the survey team!"

22 A FEW MINUTES LATER...

WE'D BEST HURRY. THEY'RE LOOKING A MITE UNCOMFORTABLE OVER THERE.

Moments later, the dinghy bumped gently against the remains of the ice floe. Sally, Benji and Rascal helped the relieved survey team (and the penguins) into the inflatable.

Spike's voice came over Sally's radio. *"Have you got everyone aboard? We'll need to tow you over to solid ice. Over."*

"Hi, Spike," replied Sally. "Yes, all aboard – and you'd better get us out of here pronto. It looks like Captain Claw is preparing to dive. We don't want him coming after us..."

Benji stared at the disappearing submarine. "How does Spike know he won't get far?"

Rascal nodded. "Orcas may be tough and mean; but they ain't no match for a submarine."

Murdoch's voice came over the radio. *"Any minute now, yon chicken-livered pussycat will find something worse than orcas down there... and unless I'm very much mistaken – yes, here they come!"*

SUFFERING CATFISH!

The Action Dogs and the rescued survey team cheered as Captain Claw's submarine plunged back into the sea with the sperm whale snapping at its tail.

"Well, I guess we don't have to worry about Captain Claw for a while," said Sally, "and Spike says the Antarctic base is sending snowmobiles to fetch the survey team. But we'll still have to pick up the *Sea Dog* and then take care of the heater-things Katmanchew already has working."

"No problem," said Benji cheerfully. "We can do all that with the Bonecopter."

"Sure, but we have to get to the Bonecopter first, and it's miles away! We haven't got the Dogsled any more, so I'm afraid it's..."

BRILLIANT! – WALKIES!!

23 ON THE ICE, SOMETIME LATER

Murdoch finished attaching the demolition charge to the last of Katmanchew's katio heaters. Seven of the mighty machines had already been blown to smithereens. He plugged the radio-controlled detonator into the high explosive charge, walked away to where the Bonecopter stood and climbed aboard.

The moment the door was closed, Sally took off. Murdoch, Spike, Benji and Rascal stared out of the cockpit windows. Benji was practically bouncing up and down with impatience. "Come on, Murdoch – blow it up!"

Murdoch gave him a stony look. "I'm waiting until we have a wee bit of distance before I set off the explosion – I used a fair sized charge for this one... All right, here we go: three...two...one..."

ZERO!

Sally looked over her shoulder and smiled. "Well, that's the last of them."

"Aye," said Murdoch. "Rascal and I can bring the Bonecopter back here once we've dropped the *Sea Dog* and what's left of the Dogsled back at base, and do a clear-up. The materials we salvage from yon katio heaters will come in very handy for making new machines for us..."

"Hold on..." Sally held up a paw and listened to her radio for a moment. "According to the scientists at the Antarctic base, the temperature around here is already falling. The sea is starting to freeze again."

"That won't be good news for Captain Claw," said Spike with grim satisfaction. "He'll be stuck underwater with a very angry whale..."

"...and he will not be a happy kitty," said Benji. "Serves him right."

"Time to go home," said Sally.

Murdoch slapped his forehead. "Ach, no! Home – that reminds me..."

"Never mind, Murdoch," said Sally. She eased her collar. "Phew! I don't know about anybody else, but I reckon rescuing people from ice floes and fighting cats on submarines is thirsty work – I'm parched! Have we got anything to drink on board?"

"Aye." Murdoch started rooting around in the icebox. "We have Cocker Cola, Ginger Beagle and milkshake."

"What flavour milkshake?"

Murdoch checked the label. "Gravy flavour."

"All right," said Sally, licking her lips, "I'll have a large glass of that, please – and NO ICE!"

24 KATMANCHEW'S SECRET HIDEOUT IN TIBET
DO YOU MEAN TO TELL ME, KATNIP, THAT CAPTAIN CLAW HAS BUNGLED YET AGAIN?
REGRETTABLY, IT IS SO, GREAT MASTER.
CURSES!

The Napoleon of crime clambered from his bath. "It seems I am surrounded by numbskulls! And once again, the Action Dogs have escaped my clutches. Mark my words, Katnip – they say every dog has its day; but soon, my enemies will find their days are numbered! Because next time..."

SURVIVE...

TERROR IN SPACE

The conniving Katmanchew has set a spaceship on a collision course with a brand-new Space Hotel full of super-rich celebrities. It's time for the Action Dogs to blast off to the rescue in the Dog Starship! But Welfare Officer Brick is inspecting the pound – so it looks like the Action Dogs are firmly grounded.

Can the Dogs escape in time to stop a cosmic katastrophe, or will it all blow up in their faces...?

ISBN 9781409520344

AND DON'T MISS MORE CANINE CAPERS IN...

OCEAN OF PERIL

ISBN 9781409520191

AND **THE HOWLING INFERNO**

ISBN 9781409520320

ADD TO YOUR COLLECTION!

SNIFF OUT TWO MORE EXTRA-SPECIAL GAME CARDS BY HEADING TO THE ACTION DOGS WEBSITE NOW!

WWW.ACTIONDOGSONLINE.COM

Plus there's more info on your favourite canines and the world's most evil kitties, and unmissable downloads.

For more fun reads check out WWW.FICTION.USBORNE.COM

First published in the UK in 2012 by Usborne Publishing Ltd., Usborne House, 83-85 Saffron Hill, London EC1N 8RT, England. www.usborne.com

Illustrations by Martin Chatterton.

A CIP catalogue record for this book is available from the British Library.

ISBN 9781409520337 JFMAM JASOND/12 02854/1

Printed in Dongguan, Guangdong, China.